One Day in the Life of Bubble Gum

Written and Illustrated by fourth-grade students of
Mt. Horeb Intermediate Center in Mt. Horeb, Wisconsin

SCHOLASTIC INC.
New York Toronto London Auckland Sydney
Mexico City New Delhi Hong Kong

ISBN 0-439-36886-3

12 11 10 9 8 7 6 5 4 3 2 1   00 01 02 03 04

Printed in the U.S.A.   08

First Printing, July 2001

Meet the Authors

There once lived a piece of plain bubble gum,
who lived a very plain and boring life.
Then one day, his life changed.

He was sitting in the candy box
next to a lollipop, like he always did, when a
hand reached in and grabbed him.

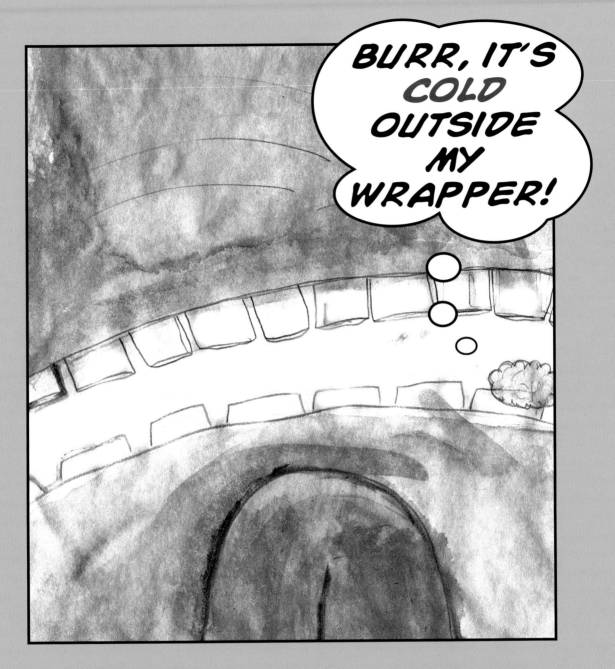

It picked him up, took off his wrapper, and popped him into a little girl's mouth.

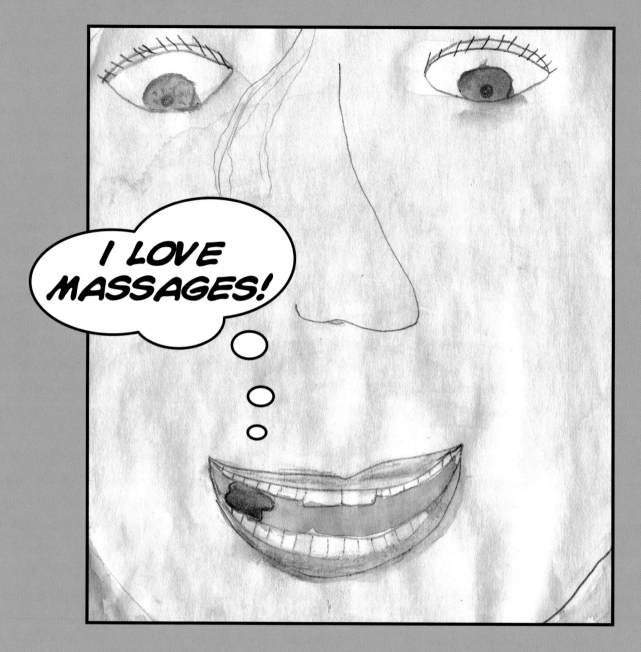

The next thing the gum felt was teeth chomping down on him. It made him feel good to know that he was wanted.

Meanwhile, outside the mouth,
the little girl and her mother were on their way
to the park for a picnic.

When they reached the park, they chose to sit
on a park bench. It was time to eat, so the
little girl took the gum out of her mouth and
stuck it under the bench.

The gum waited patiently for over an hour,
but the little girl didn't come back to get him.
All he could do was stick there and watch
feet go by him on the sidewalk.

A park maintenance worker named Bob walked up to the bench and started to scrape off the paint. He scraped quick and hard under the bench and sent the gum flying onto the sidewalk.

A businessman walking in the park stepped on the gum, and it stuck to the bottom of his shoe.

He walked to the street, flagged down a
taxi cab, and headed for the center of the city
with the gum tagging along.

The taxi drove several miles and pulled up
in front of a huge building.
As the man stepped out of the taxi, the gum
fell off his shoe and onto the sidewalk.

Just then, a small, golden bird glided over
the heads of the people on the sidewalk.
Out of the corner of her eye, she saw the
not-so-pink bubble gum.

Thinking that the gum could be used to build her nest, she picked it up in her tiny little beak and flew off towards the park.

As she soared over the park, she saw the rest of her flock and heard her mate calling her. She opened her mouth to respond, and the gum fell to the ground.

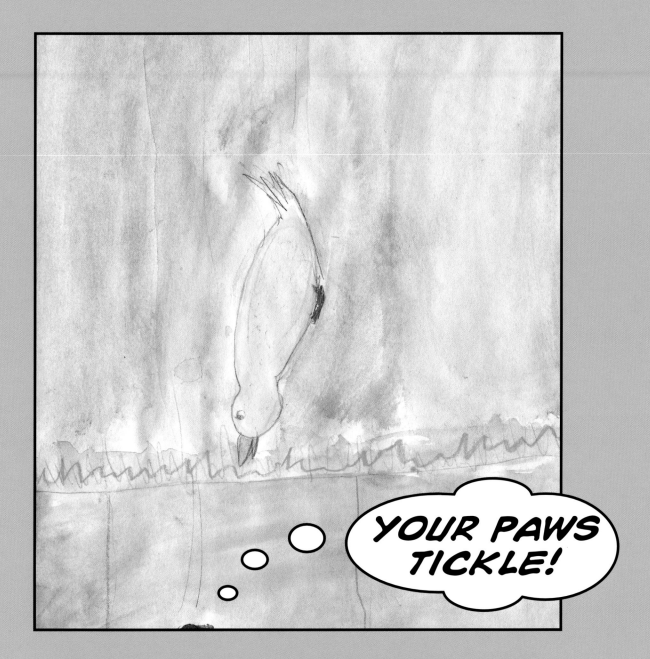

She dove to retrieve her find, but she was too late. A foraging squirrel saw the gum land and snatched it up in his furry front paws. The bird flew sadly back to her flock.

The squirrel proudly held his prize
in the air and took a nibble to see if it tasted
as good as it smelled.

Sitting in the grass and admiring the gum,
the squirrel had caught the attention of a small,
but ornery dog named Smoky.

Smoky barked at the squirrel.
The squirrel ran away, and Smoky started to
chase him, but stopped. Smoky saw the
bubble gum that the squirrel had dropped.

Smoky sniffed at the gum curiously.
He bit it and started chewing.
The gum stuck in his teeth.

Smoky walked over to his owner and tried to bark. All that came out was a gurgle, because of the gum.

Smoky's owner asked,
"What are you chewing on, Smoky?"
The owner opened Smoky's mouth, picked out
the gum, and stuck it back under the bench.

The next day, the little girl and her mom
came back to the park for a walk.
The little girl wanted to rest, so they both sat
on a newly painted bench.

The little girl looked under the bench,
and sure enough, the gum was still there!
When her mother wasn't looking,
she put the gum back into her mouth.

As she chewed, she thought to herself,
"Hey, this gum tastes better than yesterday!
I wonder how it got so good?"

Kids Are Authors®

Books written by children for children

The Kids Are Authors® Competition was established in 1986 to encourage children and to become involved in the creative process of writing. Since then, thousands of children have written and illustrated books as participants in the Kids Are Authors® Competition. The winning books in the annual competition are published by Scholastic Inc. and are distributed by Scholastic Book Fairs throughout the United States.

For more information:

Kids Are Authors®
Scholastic Book Fairs
PO Box 958411
Lake Mary, FL 32795-8411

or visit our web site at:
www.scholasticbookfairs.com